The
When My Mother & Father Forsake Me...

Psalm 27:10

Workbook

The WHEN MY MOTHER & FATHER FORSAKE ME...

Psalm 27:10

Five G.R.A.C.E. Steps for Healing Parental Rejection & Hurts

Workbook

A. Jesus Wrighter, M.Div.

Los Angeles

When My Mother & Father Forsake Me…Workbook
Copyright © 2012 by Food for Faith Publications

This title is also available as a Food for Faith Audio product. Visit www.foodforfaith.org/audiobooks for more information.

Requests for information should be addressed to:

Food for Faith Publications
P.O. Box 88445
Los Angeles, CA 90009
www.foodforfaith.org

All scripture verses cited in this book used by permission. Versions included:

CEV *Contemporary English Version*, New York: American Bible Society (1995)
GW *God's Word Translation*, Grand Rapids: World Publishing, Inc. (1995)
KJV *King James Version*
MSG *The Message*, Wheaton, IL: Tyndale House Publishers (1979)
NAB *New American Bible*, Chicago: Catholic Press (1970)
NASB *New American Standard Bible*, Anaheim, CA: Foundation Press (1973)
NCV *New Century Version*, Dallas: World Bibles (1991)
NIV *New International Version*, Colorado Springs: International Bible Society (1978, 1984)
NLT *New Living Translation*, Wheaton, IL: Tyndale House Publishers (1996)
TEV *Today's English Version*, New York: American Bible Society (1992)

This book is the proprietary work of Food for Faith Publications. Many terms in this book, including the title, are trademarks of Food for Faith Publications. Any unauthorized use of this copyrighted material or use of any of these terms in relation to goods and/or services (including seminars, workshops, training programs, classes, etc.) is prohibited without the express written permission of the owner.

All rights reserved, including the right to reproduce this book or portions thereof in any form whatsoever.

FOOD FOR FAITH and the portrayal of an open bible on a plate flanked by a knife and fork are trademarks of Food for Faith Publications.

Manufactured in the United States of America

ISBN 978-0-9770845-0-0

For my daughter, Johanna, from whose life I am daily learning the beauty of grace. You are the fulfillment of the promise.

Acknowledgments

Thank you, Pascale, for working hard to help me succeed.

Thank to my invisible agent, editor, and publicist: Yahweh, Jesus, and the Holy Spirit.

Table of Contents

Overview 11

PART 1: ANATOMY 15
1 – Introduction to Prejection 17
2 – Soul Maps 21
3 – The Preject Test... 25
4 – Creating Your Genogram 29
5 – 7 A's in Parenting 35
6 – Love, Care & Skill.. 41
7 – Naked Speaking Spirits... 45
8 – Dissatisfaction Guaranteed.. 49

PART 2: PATHOLOGY 51
9 – The Mephibosheth Mandate 53
10 – Preject Syndrome 55
11 – Preject Pathologies 61

PART 3: G.R.A.C.E. 65
12 – Heal Yourself! 67
13 – Grieve 69
16 – Release 79
19 – Accept 89
20 – Comfort 91
21 – Establish 95

PART 4: SIGNS 111
28 – The Orphan Heart 113
29 – 10 Commandments for Prejects 117
30 – 40 Parenting Skills for Prejects 119

Appendix 125
About the Author 127
Send Us Your Story! 128

Overview

This workbook will help you to examine the causes and effects of parental rejection and disconnection in your own life as well as the lives of others you know. It will also guide you through the steps for overcoming parental rejection and help you break down the barriers blocking you from accessing your full potentialities by leading you through prayers, exercises, and encounters.

As a practical compliment to *When My Mother & Father Forsake Me...*, this workbook is intended to provoke you to think critically about your family structure, your relationship with your parents, and their impact on your current ability to function at optimal levels. In these pages you will be challenged and engaged to examine the causes of parental rejection and its impact on both the children and adults in your household, work through steps to overcome it, and create preventative measures to protect yourself from forming future generational households impacted by parental rejection. This workbook is uniquely designed to equip parents, students, teachers, spiritual aids, foster parents and foster children with the tools necessary to overcome the limiting and pernicious effects of parental rejection.

The workbook's objectives are:

1. To introduce you to the conceptual foundations of parental acceptance and rejection theory (PART).

2. To impart to you specific steps that can be taken to overcome the effects of parental rejection in any child's or adult's life.

3. To assist you in developing a personal family structure and parental behavior theory that will prevent parental rejection in your future families and curtail it in your current families.

Like its companion text, this workbook is also organized into four parts:

Part 1 – Anatomy

Laying a Foundation. This introductory section of the workbook is designed to immerse you in preject memories to reconnect you with their root so it can be eradicated. You will complete a genogram, write a reflection on your findings, and complete several exercises, including a preject self-assessment, that require recall of painful family experiences.

Topics:

- Introduction to Prejection: Parental rejection defined
- Soul Maps: The Four Stages of Brokenness
- The Preject Test: Cracked, Broken, or Shattered?
- Creating Your Genogram: from antiquity to present
- The Seven A's in Parenting
- Love, Care & Skill: The *Bear* Necessities
- Naked Speaking Spirits & Silent Shadow Talkers: The Theo-psychology of Disconnection
- Dissatisfaction Guaranteed: Personal Impacts

Part 2 – Pathology

Prejects in Society & the Culture of Rejection. This section of the workbook guides you through the process of determining and defining the impact parental rejection has had, and continues to have, on your life.

You are introduced to Ronal P. Rohner's research and my analysis of preject pathology.

Topics:

- The Mephibosheth Mandate: Handle With Care
- Preject Syndrome
- Preject Pathologies

Part 3 – G.R.A.C.E.

Prejects, Personal Responsibility, & Self-Transformation. This section of the workbook focuses exclusively on the understanding and application of the Five G.R.A.C.E. Steps. Through a combination of external source materials, YouTube® videos, readings, written self-reflections, role-playing, and phone calls, you are taken step by step through the difficulties and rewards of G.R.A.C.E. You will establish a Confrontation Day™, customize your unique healing plan, create your Five Family Statements™, and begin taking measurable steps to transformation.

Topics:

- Heal Yourself!: Applying the G.R.A.C.E. Steps
- **G**rieve
- **R**elease
- **A**ccept
- **C**omfort
- **E**stablish

Part 4 – Signs

The Hallmarks of a PRO Life. The final section of the workbook is comprised of self-discussions, reflection exercises, and considerable reorientation about the nature of the human soul, parental relationships, and the psychological, social, economic and political impacts of parental rejection in contemporary life. You are also encouraged to think about your future family life choices as they relate to their impacts on a world of increasingly limited emotional resources. You create channels for transmitting your PRO worldview to future generations, and discover opportunities to connect and participate with a global community of PROs.

Topics:

- The Orphan Heart & the Journey to Sonship
- The Ten Commandments for Prejects
- Forty Parenting Skills for Prejects

Part 1

Anatomy

Laying a Foundation

- Introduction to Prejection: Parental rejection defined
- Soul Maps: The Four Stages of Brokenness
- The Preject Test: Three Degrees of Soul Damage
- Creating Your Genogram: from antiquity to present
- The Seven A's in Parenting
- Naked Speaking Spirits & Silent Shadow Talkers: The Theo-
- psychology of Disconnection
- Love, Care & Skill: The *Bear* Necessities
- Dissatisfaction Guaranteed: Personal Impacts

Chapter 1

Introduction to Prejection: Parental Rejection Defined

Parental rejection occurs when a child feels physically or emotionally disconnected from and rejected by a parent. Triggers for this feeling of rejection can range from one cataclysmic incident of abuse, abandonment, neglect, or absence, to a palpable atmosphere of non-acceptance constructed over time by consistently expressed attitudes of disapproval, annoyance, and disappointment.

Every preject has a memory of their defining preject moment, when they became aware that they were not getting from their parent what they needed to affirm their life and existence. Articulating that moment is the key to initiating the healing process through it.

When we express something as amorphous as a feeling of rejection, it brings it out of the undefinable, nebulous place in our psyche into a controlled, definable place where we can examine, overpower, and confine it to impotence.

Take as much time as you need to fully, exhaustively chronicle your first preject memory. Detail what happened and how you felt.

_____
_____
_____

Describe in detail your feelings, your observations, and your understanding of yourself and your parent in the context you were in at the time.

At the time, what did you think your future would be like in your family, and in life, in light of that preject moment.

Chapter 2

Soul Maps

The **4 Stages of Brokenness:**

Prejection can happen in any stage of childhood, and produces variants of project syndrome depending on the developmental stage in which the prejection began and concluded.

1. ***Womb*** – the embryonic months, when everything that makes us who we are, cells and words, is being poured into us, shaping us, defining us, creating and installing our potentialities.
2. ***B.I.T.*** (baby, infant, toddler) – the pre-school years, when everything should be done for us. *Want others to do everything for me. Think the world owes me. Infantile behavior. Self-centered. It's all about me.*
3. ***Pre-adolescent*** – the elementary school years, when we should be trained to become independent. *Won't trust anybody to do anything for me. I'll do everything for myself. Can't trust authorities or leaders. Can't trust Yahweh.*
4. ***Adolescent*** – the junior and senior high school years, when we should be taught to positively impact the lives of others. *Won't do anything for anybody else unless there is something in it for me. Deceptive. Take advantage of others by my skill and ability to help. Leverage everything. Nothing in life is free.*

People who were rejected in the womb by a parent present a noticeably different persona to the world than those who were rejected as toddlers or adolescents. The childhood stage in which one was rejected also shapes one's perception and understanding of that rejection as well.

In what stage were you broken?: _____

Recall the ways in which you interacted with your family members and peers in that stage, before and after your primary rejection moment/memory.

_____
_____
_____
_____
_____
_____
_____
_____
_____
_____
_____
_____
_____
_____
_____

Compare it to the ways in which you interact with them now.

_____
_____
_____
_____
_____
_____
_____
_____
_____
_____
_____
_____
_____
_____
_____

Are there any ways in which you still function today as a creature of that life stage, still seeking what you were supposed to get during that stage? If yes, how? If no, how?

Chapter 3

The Preject Test

The **Three Degrees of Soul Damage**:

Prejection damages our soul and separates us from our parents and ourselves. The degree to which that damage and disconnect occurs is determined by the nature and intensity of the projecting behavior we experienced most from our projecting parent or parents. The three degrees of soul damage and relational disconnect visible among prejects, along with the behaviors that produce them, are:

1. *The Shattered Soul*: all forms of extreme **abuse** (physical, sexual, verbal, emotional) lead to a *shattered* soul. This degree of soul damage often results in institutionalization. Many incarcerated or committed prejects are abuse victims who have been unable to reconcile the truth points of their abuse with their understanding of justice.

2. *The Broken Soul*: all forms of marginal **abandonment** (distance, withdrawal, withholding, occlusion, emotional and physical) lead to a *broken* soul. This degree of soul damage often results in the neurotic behaviors that compromise relationships, rendering them untenable and painful. Many divorcees, the chronically unemployed, and the clinically depressed are abandonment victims who unwittingly, habitually recreate disconnection in unconscious attempts to understand and heal it.

3. *The Cracked Soul*: all forms of benign **neglect** (refusal to impart care, wisdom, instruction, unavailability, business) lead to *cracked* souls. This degree of soul damage often results in compliant social behavior void of any real joy, meaning, or purpose. Many people who accept and maintain dissatisfactory relationships in most corners of their lives are victims of neglect who would rather have something less than perfect, than nothing at all.

Surf to **http://theprejecttest.com** and you will find a free self-assessment featuring 30 quick, multiple choice questions about your relationship with your parents that should take you about five minutes to complete.

The results of this assessment will help you to identify and determine the severity of the damage inflicted on your soul by the rejection of your parent(s), and provide some basic guidance and direction to begin the process of healing yourself and protecting your own children from a similar fate and life. Naming and confronting our degree of soul damage is the first step toward reclaiming the connected life God intended from the beginning.

Identify and record your degree of soul damage. Are you cracked, broken, or shattered?

_____

Detail the ways in which abuse, abandonment, and/or neglect have defined your relationship with one of both of your parents, and impacted your relationships and life today.

_____
_____
_____
_____
_____
_____
_____
_____
_____
_____
_____
_____
_____
_____
_____
_____
_____
_____

The Preject Test

Write specific, detailed accounts of these behaviors by your parent/s, along with the specific feelings they aroused in you at the time, and the feelings they produce in you today.

Chapter 4

Creating Your Genogram

From antiquity to present

Genealogies were used by Yahweh in scripture to show us the generational connections between Jesus, David, and Abraham. Like genealogies, genograms can also help us to recognize family patterns of prejection that might not be otherwise obvious.

Complete the simple genogram on the following page using these basic rules, paying special attention to the parental relationships in all generations depicted:

- Males are noted by squares, females by circles.
- A solid line connects married couples; a dotted line connects unmarried couples.
- Broken relationships (including those broken early in childhood) are marked with two slashes and a date of occurrence above the slashes.
- Draw lines between each parent and child, depicting their relationship:
  - Draw one jagged line for a hostile relationship.
  - Draw two jagged lines for a violent or abusive relationship.
  - Draw no line if there has never been a relationship.
  - Draw one straight line for a plain relationship.
  - Draw two straight lines for a strong, close relationship.
- When completed, examine the simple genogram for patterns.

When My Mother & Father Forsake Me...Workbook

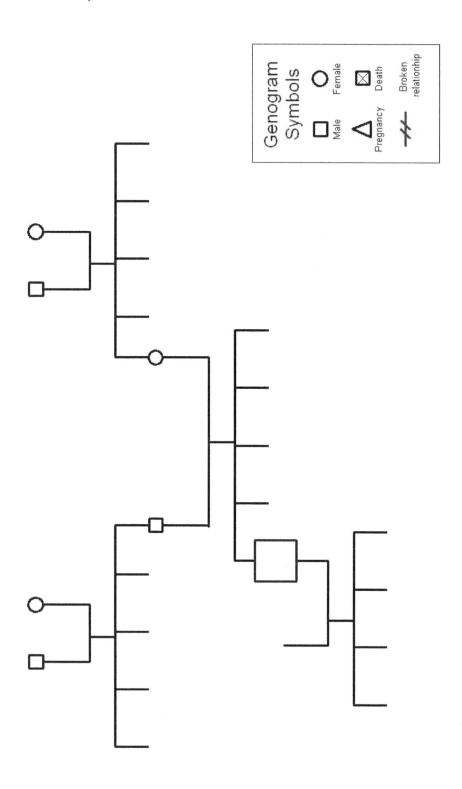

Creating Your Genogram

What basic relationship patterns, if any, do you notice in your simple genogram?

What generational patterns, if any, do you notice in the relationships between fathers and their children? Are they mostly close? Broken? Describe in detail.

What generational patterns, if any, do you notice in the relationships between mothers and their children? Are they mostly close? Hostile? Describe in detail.

Examine and describe any gender or birth order relationship patterns. e.g. Do firstborns have consistently different relationships than secondborns? Do mothers have close relationships with sons but hostile relationships with daughters? Describe in detail.

Where does your relationship with your rejecting parent fit in the patterns you've observed Is it unique or consistent with established patterns? Explain in detail.

Chapter 5

How Many A's in Parenting?

The Seven A's in Parenting

In the various models of parenting employed throughout the world and across cultures from antiquity to the present, there has been a coherent group of parenting conventions that has consistently produced stellar results in creating a sense of belonging and acceptance among children. I have labeled those conventions the Seven A's in Parenting. When used effectively they wield great power to shape a life future, and impart confidence to children:

- **Accept** – embrace fully, flaws & all, without comparisons.
- **Address** – speak to and communicate with him/her often.
- **Acknowledge** – see him/her fully. Recognize their full presence.
- **Admire** – communicate to the child that you like what you see.
- **Affirm** – communicate that what you see in him/her is good.
- **Approve** – verbally endorse his/her efforts & accomplishments.
- **Admonish** – verbally correct the child when s/he goes astray.

Which A's were present in your childhood? **For each A describe in detail the parental behaviors and attitudes that expressed that A in your childhood. If the A was missing describe in detail what parental behaviors and attitudes replaced that missing A in your childhood. Finally, describe the continuing impact of the presence or absence of each A on your life and self-esteem today, as you understand it.**

Accept:

Address:

How Many A's in Parenting?

Acknowledge:

Admire:

Affirm:

Approve:

Admonish:

Chapter 6

Naked Speaking Spirits & Silent Shadow Talkers

The Theopsychology of Disconnection

Access, online, and listen to your complimentary edition of part one of Earl Middleton's audio program, *Cracking the Code of Silence* (http://sermon.net/earlmiddleton/sermonid/2416359/type/audio) in which he shares insights from the Holy Spirit, and the work of behavioral psychologists and linguists, about the lethal power of silence in human communities, and its dual role as both an agent and product of parental rejection.

Although we were all created to be naked speaking spirits, communicating in total transparency with Yahweh and each other, virtually all parents who reject their children live and parent in hiding as silent shadow talkers who never fully reveal themselves to their children.

Nakedness requires vulnerability, but rejecting parents are so damaged and fearful of further damage that they can't risk vulnerability. Without the nakedness needed to communicate the seven A's of parenting they end up parenting from their shadow, leaving their children in the dark, feeling rejected, *other*, and excluded from parent's inner life.

Describe the level of parental transparency in your childhood household. How much did your parents let you see and know of their inner and/or past life?

_____
_____
_____

How much of their flaws, their nakedness, were they willing to reveal, or did they try to hide? Provide three specific examples.

How comfortable/uncomfortable were your parents in sharing conversations about their feelings with you? Give three examples.

Chapter 7

Love, Care & Skill: The *Bear* Necessities

What it Takes to Fully Support a Child

What is the relationship among love, care, and skill in communicating full parental acceptance to a child?

Children are not born with the instinctual knowledge that they are loved. That reality has to be communicated by the parents during the bonding and attachment phase of the child's early development. And that communication does not take place accidentally nor automatically, but intentionally.

The two primary tools Yahweh puts in the hands of parents to equip them to communicate this love to their children are *care* and *skill*. Care is the ability to place focused, uninterrupted attention on a child; to be fully available emotionally, physically, and financially. Skill is the acquired and applied knowledge bank utilized by parents to move their child from one place or stage in childhood to the next.

Care and skill do not come hardwired or pre-installed in parents. Both must be acquired, developed, and protected by parents on purpose. While the absence of care and skill do not necessarily indicate a lack of parental love, the presence of both does not guarantee parental success. What they do guarantee is that children will know they are accepted.

Describe your parents' care ability. How did they fail or succeed in demonstrating care? What helped or hindered them?

_____

_____

Describe your parents' skill level. How did they fail or succeed in utilizing parenting skill to help you grow physically, spiritually, emotionally, and intellectually?

Where and how did they receive their parenting training? Did they continue to acquire parenting skills while they were parenting you?

_____
_____
_____
_____
_____

What care abilities and parenting skills have you acquired from your parents, either good or bad?

_____
_____
_____
_____
_____
_____
_____
_____
_____
_____

Which abilities and skills seen in your parents have you decided to utilize with your own children? Which have you decided not to use?

_____
_____
_____
_____
_____
_____
_____
_____
_____
_____

Chapter 8

Dissatisfaction Guaranteed

The Preject Condition

If you've been prejected you'll be dissatisfied in life to a degree that is not common or evident in the lives of those raised in full acceptance.

According to the Apostle James when we try to use things to fill us up we ask amiss to consume it...on our desires (*James 4:3*). Asking amiss is about consumption, and consumption is for filling. But the things we are asking for were not designed to fill us. We can never be *fulfilled* (filled up) until we are full, and satisfied; and that can't happen until we get our cistern-souls healed and the leaking stopped.

Many prejects try to get that feeling of *fulfillment* or *fullness* by cramming their lives with things, but never find fulfillment because it only comes from Spirit, not things; and Spirit won't and can't stay in a broken cistern-soul vessel.

Prejection breaks our cistern-soul and keeps us empty. The difference between satisfied living and empty living is: when we're satisfied we don't want or crave *anything*, no matter how much or how little we have. We are full not from things, but from relationship with our Source, Yahweh, and the people He created and placed in our lives.

Describe in detail your life cravings. What have you pursued to fill you up?

_____

_____

Identify a season when you felt satisfied. How long did it last? If you can't, describe what you imagine satisfaction to be and feel like.

Part 2

Pathology

Prejects in Society & the Culture of Rejection

> When I was 15 and going to the school psychologist's office every day to try to make sense out of the pain in my life and understand the alienation I was feeling, I would have snapped up a book like this.
> ~ *A. Jesus Wrighter*

- The Mephibosheth Mandate: Handle With Care
- Preject Syndrome
- Preject Pathologies

Chapter 9

The Mephibosheth Mandate

Mephibosheth's Mandate: Handle with care! It's very easy for prejecting parents to drop their baby.

Dropping the Baby - a metaphor for poor parenting by virtue of lack of skills (knowledge), or lack of care (inner availability or attention; an inability to see).

Mephibosheth is the poster child for prejects. He was broken because and when he was dropped as a toddler (*2 Samuel 4:4*).[1] He spent the rest of his life crippled by that one experience until David decided to bless him, helping him overcome the incident (which meant no longer managing life *from* or *out of* that damaging moment, but rather living life *through* and *past* it). Like Mephibosheth, many prejects are dropped as toddlers by parents who mishandle them; Mephibosheth's mandate is a challenge to all parents: handle every child with care, because when you mishandle and drop a child, s/he can be crippled for life.

Describe how you were dropped as a child. Were you mishandled by skill or care? How so? How did it cripple you?

_____

_____

---

[1] *2 Samuel 4:4* (NLT) (Saul's son Jonathan had a son named Mephibosheth, who was crippled as a child. He was five years old when Saul and Jonathan were killed at the battle of Jezreel. When news of the battle reached the capital, the child's nurse grabbed him and fled. But she fell and dropped him as she was running, and he became crippled as a result.)

What *crutches* have you used to help you manage your disability?

Has there been a *David* in your life? If so, how has s/he blessed you?

Chapter 10

Preject Syndrome

Preject Syndrome manifests in a constellation of behaviors and attitudes unique to people who have been rejected by a parent. Those behaviors and attitudes are:

1. *Hostility* – anger and aggression are often coping strategies for loss. Elizabeth Kubler-Ross identified anger as the second stage of grief, and the English word *anger* comes from an Old Norse word, *angr*, which means *grief*. Prejects become hostile and aggressive when awareness of their parental loss begins to grip their hearts and souls.
2. *Dependency* – when a child loses the protection, direction, and nurture parents have been charged to impart, they become clingy and dependent upon the nearest parental figure as a way of compensating for that loss and in search of protection from future loss or the horrific outcomes that loss might imply.
3. *Low Self-Esteem* – children rejected by a parent internalize the rejection as a sign that they are unworthy, insufficient, and defective. Once those values have been accepted and embellished by corroborating behavior, it is difficult to reverse. This low self-esteem leads children to identify and connect with their baser self and the base elements of their society.

4. *Emotional Instability* – parental rejection and loss leave children without an inner governor for their emotions. With no one to model appropriate expressions and control of emotions, children are left with no idea of how to handle their raw emotions and as a result swing between the feral and the subdued. Moments that demand strong emotion are often met with indifference, while more mundane moments are invested with exuberance.
5. *Emotional Unresponsiveness* – when a child is rejected by a parent the pain of the loss often leaves the child numb and determined to protect him/herself from future pain. So, the child shuts down emotionally, not allowing others to get close enough to hurt them. This guarded protection stance begins to overtake the personality the longer the prejection is left untreated, so that prejects can become emotional islands. Even in the midst of community with a battery of relationships, few, if any, people will ever be able to say that they truly know the preject.
6. *Negative Worldview* – the pain of parental rejection and loss usually leaves the preject with a pretty grim outlook on life. If one's parent can reject and hurt them, then what about the rest of the world with no vested or biological reason to care? Cynicism, cold-heartedness, and pessimism are the major inculcated responses to this kind of hurt. This is also in large part responsible for the generational nature of prejection. Negativity is a contagion and the children of prejects are often infected with it unbeknownst to the preject parent, because the iniquities of the parents really do find their way into the lives of their kids.

Describe in detail if and how each component of preject syndrome has manifest in your life. How soon after your 'preject moment' or baby dropping did these behaviors and attitudes begin to show up in your life. How have your family, classmates, colleagues, friends, and lovers responded to the components of preject syndrome evident in your life? What efforts have you made to mute or eliminate these behaviors and attitudes from your life? If any, how effective have those efforts been?

Hostility:

Dependency:

Low Self-Esteem:

Emotional Instability:

Emotional Unresponsiveness:

Negative Worldview:

Chapter 11

Preject Pathologies

5 Pathologies that Identify Prejects

How does prejection distort life, and what are the telltale signs that someone is a preject? Scripture gives us a picture of five categories of life distortions that Jesus came to correct. All of them are rooted in parental rejection. All 40 preject pathologies fall into one of these following five categories:

1. ***Broke*** – There is a strong direct relationship between prejection and poverty. Prejects often have plenty of inner resources but little success converting them into money, because money lack is a product of poverty of spirit. **Record the income seasons of your life and the incidents responsible for any/all fluctuations.**

_____
_____
_____
_____
_____
_____
_____
_____
_____
_____
_____
_____
_____
_____

2. ***Broken Hearted*** – souls contain hearts. When souls dysfunction from damage they spill hearts, breaking them and wasting the power they contain. **Describe your energy level when faced with a hard task and how you motivate yourself to eventually engage the task.**

_____
_____
_____
_____
_____
_____
_____
_____
_____
_____
_____
_____
_____
_____
_____
_____
_____

3. ***Bound*** – people stuck in the past, whose life transmissions only go in reverse, who have difficulty with forgiveness and find it hard to let go of hurts, are bound (to the past). **Detail all you can remember of your last conversation with a significant other. How much of it is about the past?**

_____
_____
_____
_____
_____
_____
_____

4. ***Blind*** – people who cannot see, even though they have eyes, are beset by spiritual blindness. **Using hindsight, describe three things you were unable to see even though they were right in front of you and others were able to see them.**

5. ***Bruised*** – people who have been crushed, oppressed; unable to rise (which is the goal of fatherhood: to raise up) have been so bruised that they cannot function effectively. **Describe in detail who/what (if any) has been keeping you down throughout your life.**

Part 3

G.R.A.C.E.

Prejects, Personal Responsibility, & Self Transformation

- Heal Yourself!: Applying the G.R.A.C.E. Steps
  - **G**rieve
  - **R**elease
  - **A**ccept
  - **C**omfort
  - **E**stablish

Chapter 12

Heal Yourself!

Applying the G.R.A.C.E. Steps

"Physician, heal thyself!" The onlookers mocked Jesus with those words. That tone and sentiment survives in the body of Christ today. The very idea of self-healing is derided among Christians, but like David, who encouraged himself in the Lord, that is exactly what Yahweh expects us to do when it comes to inner healing. We have been equipped and empowered by Yahweh to speak to ourselves and watch His word bring about healing.

In this section of the workbook we will take personal responsibility for our own self transformation by applying the five G.R.A.C.E. steps to our unique parental relationship situations.

To get maximum impact complete each exercise thoroughly before moving on to the next one. If you feel stuck on an exercise give yourself time to get unstuck. You may have to labor over an exercise for several days before finally breaking through to completion. Give the Holy Spirit time to work with and through your damaged soul. Some healings manifest immediately, others require time to transition into the visible realm.

Remember that the key to successfully completing these G.R.A.C.E. step exercises is to consistently speak the word of God to your soul, and articulate verbally the victory Jesus died to give you.

Chapter 13

Grieve

Exercise 1

The word *grieve* means to lose. When we lose something valuable we experience pain. The natural human response to pain is to jettison it, or if that fails, then to bury it. In both instances we are attempting to forget our pain, and by extension, our loss. We improve our chances for successful grieving by following these healthy steps to forgetting:

1) ***Review***. I must look with my whole being at the thing or incident I am trying to forget. I must look at every aspect of it and examine it to see what I may have missed before. I must get a full picture before I can fully forget.

2) ***Resent***. I must resent with my whole being the thing or incident I am trying to forget. The English word *resent* comes from the French word *sentir* which means *to feel*. To *resent* is to *re-feel*. Reviewing helps me to intellectually reconnect, but resenting allows me to viscerally reconnect. I must remember how the thing or incident made or makes me feel before I can forget it viscerally.

3) ***Release***. I must release with my whole being the thing or incident I am trying to forget. This is the component that actuates true forgetting, and will be explained further in the next chapter. To forget I must verbally release the thing or incident.

Too many people try to release their loss and pain without fully reviewing and resenting it. **Write a detailed review of your parental loss, then fully describe the feelings of resentment associated with it.**

Chapter 14

Grieve

Exercise 2

When a nursing mother generates more milk than she can feed her child she avoids painful engorgement by using a breast pump to remove the milk, and then stores it in a bottle for later use. This process is called *expressing*. It is also the perfect description of the grief process.

Grieving prejects are engorged with pain (cf. chapter 6 in *When My Mother & Father Forsake Me...* for an explanation of the effects of grief in a preject's life), and often unaware that they are actually grieving.

Grieving is the soul's attempt to process pain through and out of the life so that we can return to normalcy. If left on the unconscious plane and to itself this process can drag on for years and diminish our lives. The first G.R.A.C.E. step calls us to take control of the grief process, accelerating it so that we eliminate the toxic pain from our lives as soon as possible and get back to enjoying life the way Yahweh intended it.

In order to do this we must express our grief the way a nursing mother expresses milk, moving our pain from one location to another.

Now that you have reconnected with your pain and have stepped again into the place of resentment about the loss of the parenting and childhood Yahweh designed all children to be affirmed and grow through, write a letter, expressing your full blown grief regarding everything in Parts 1 & 2 of this workbook, to your rejecting parent(s) and then read it out loud to yourself.

Chapter 15

Grieve

Exercise 3

In chapter 6 of *When My Mother & Father Forsake Me...* I explain the difference between passive and active grieving. The steps to active grieving, the most productive kind of grieving, are outlined below. Write a detailed response to each of these seven grief steps:

1) ***Be Afflicted*** – wretched; realize our own misery. Own up to the misery inflicted by your parental rejection. **Define your misery.**

_____
_____
_____
_____
_____
_____
_____
_____
_____
_____
_____
_____
_____
_____

2) ***Mourn*** – *pentheo*: grieve. Go beyond just acknowledging your misery; begin to feel again the pain of your rejection by revisiting every painful memory and moment in your mind, soul,

and spirit. **Describe your feelings associated with each memory.**

_____
_____
_____
_____
_____
_____
_____
_____
_____
_____
_____
_____
_____

3) *Weep* – sob, wail aloud. The more public it is, the more cathartic it is, for it validates your feelings of rejection, perhaps for the first time. **Document and/or plan moments of public weeping.**

_____
_____
_____
_____
_____
_____
_____
_____
_____
_____
_____
_____
_____

4) *Laughter to mourning* – fast. Eliminate all sources and forms of laughter and levity from your life and fully commit to the

process of grieving until it is complete. **Calendar this process. Forecast planned dates for finishing each of these seven grief steps and grieving to completion.**

_____

5) *Joy to heaviness* – downcast in look; sadness. Shift in perspective from joy to a sad heaviness that looks downward and sees, examines the worst. **Detail the worst parts of your prejection.**

_____

6) *Humble yourself* – (depression, humility) in the sight (face) of the Lord. Completely surrender to the will of Yahweh. **Define what this means in your present life context. What does it require you to do?**

_____
_____
_____
_____
_____
_____
_____
_____
_____
_____
_____
_____

7) *Exaltation* – Elevation. Responsibly maintain our new identity. **Describe in detail your vision of your new identity.**

_____
_____
_____
_____
_____
_____
_____
_____
_____
_____
_____
_____
_____
_____

Chapter 16

Release

Exercise 1

In a speech he gave at Oxford University on March 21, 2001, Michael Jackson said, "You probably weren't surprised to hear that I did not have an idyllic childhood. ...The strain and tension that exists in my relationship with my own father is well documented. ...He had great difficulty showing affection. ...He never really told me he loved me. And he never really complimented me either."

Later in that same speech Michael acknowledged his need, for his own healing, to forgive his father. How did he do it? He applied the principles of release-forgiveness. Whether your parent is present in your life, just accessible, or completely disconnected, you can take the next step in healing your soul by applying the biblical principles of forgiveness. Write your response to the instruction of each of the following steps:

1. *Acknowledge Offense* – **detail what was done and its impact on you.**

___
___
___
___
___
___

2. *Understand* – to the best of your ability, detail *your parent's* reason for behaving the way s/he did. If you don't know or can't find out, detail what you *suspect* the reason might be.

3. *Confront* (privately; verbally) – detail what you would say to your rejecting parent if s/he were sitting in front of you. Express your pain. Draw from your grief letter in Chapter 14.

4. *Release and Transfer* – imagine all your pain returned to sender. Detail how your life will change with all parental rejection pain gone.

Chapter 17

Release

Exercise 2

Confrontation Day – 70•7 – Practice

Find a picture of your prejecting parent. The closer to their age when you last felt rejected by them, the better. This will help you to practice conducting an effective parental confrontation by talking to the picture to release anger. The heart of this exercise is the opportunity to *confront* parents *in the spirit*, and release and transfer pain back to them.

Confrontation Day is the key goal in G.R.A.C.E. step 2 (*Release*). You can't fully release until you get to and through *confrontation day*. For some people this requires a lengthy time of preparation.

It *is* possible to experience inner healing by confronting dead or absent people through *visualization*. The valence in confrontation is in *your* expression of words, not in what *they* (those who hurt you) have to say. You can express words and fully release even if the offender isn't physically present. You can talk to an absent spirit and still get *healed* because healing comes from what *you* say, not what *they* say. In this exercise you're ministering healing to yourself.

Using your answer to part 3 in the previous exercise, and drawing on your grief letter from Chapter 14, create your confrontation day script. Include every detail: location; setting; wardrobe. Everything. Write what you will say; their response; your response to their response; etc. Write it how you want it to go. It's *your* script. You're in charge. **Now begin rehearsing your lines by speaking to your parent's picture.**

Release

Chapter 18

Release

Exercise 3

Confrontation Day – 70•7 – Game time

Full release of your pain, and restoration of your soul to its original state before your parental rejection, has already happened if you completed the previous exercise. Using the words of your own mouth to release your parent(s) has brought about healing. This third release exercise is really not necessary for your healing. It's only necessary to give your rejecting parent a shot at transformation and healing for him/herself; and for you to fully obey Yahweh and imitate Christ.

Confronting your parent in person gives him/her an opportunity to hear you, repent, and confess. And only through their repentance and confession can you find authentic, lasting, relationship-transforming reconciliation. Release-forgiveness only requires change in one person to make it happen (you), but reconciliation requires real change take place in two people (you, *and* your parent).

Give your rejecting parent a chance at transformation and reconciliation. **Schedule your Confrontation Day.** You set the time and place. You decide the ground rules. You establish the time limits.

Take someone with you. Enlist the help of a reliable friend or family member who will accompany you to the *Confrontation Day* site for witnessing and support. Tell them as much or as little about the purpose of the meeting as you want or need to. Insure their availability for the scheduled meeting before you contact your parent. Get a backup if necessary.

Decide how you will invite your parent to your *confrontation day* meeting. Will you call, use e-mail, text, send a letter, use a messenger? Chose the method that is least stressful and most advantageous for you.

Invite you parent(s) to the Confrontation Day meeting. Don't refer to it as confrontation day. Don't be surprised if they decline to attend. If they decline, leave the invitation open. If they accept:

Attend the meeting. Invite the presence of Yahweh before you enter the meeting room. Control your breathing. Don't be afraid of or worried about getting emotional. Station your witness close enough so you can be seen, but far enough away so you can't be heard; or outside of a closed, not locked, door, so they can come in if you call loudly for them.

Stick to your script. Don't alter it during the meeting. This is why you need to spend sufficient time writing and rehearsing it. Everything you need to say should be in there. You can't be sure of your parent's words, but you can be sure of yours.

Date: _____

Time: _____

Location: _____

Ground Rules: _____
_____

Time Limit: _____

Witness: _____

Witness Backup: _____

Witness Station: _____

Invitation Method: _____

Parent Contact Info: _____
_____

Chapter 19

Accept

The next step in overcoming parental rejection is accepting a *SPA* (*substitute parental adoption*) by a substituted spiritual family. Accepting adoption and entering into an earthly SPA parent-child relationship provides the context for your healing to take root and bloom. Wholeness implies balance and balance requires maternal *and* paternal relationships the way a stool needs four legs. In the end your spiritual relationships will outlast your biological ones if your blood relatives are not born again. Blood may be thicker than water, but spirit is stronger than blood. So a spiritual mother or father can provide even more balance for your life than an unsaved, rejecting biological parent. God honors His word, so if you have been rejected by a parent God has already sent into your life a substitute who He has equipped and anointed to pour into your life and soak from your life as well, in fulfillment of His promise in *Psalm 27:10*. It's an ancient tool utilized by Yahweh Himself in revealing His son to the world. The Heavenly Father used Joseph, a parental substitute, to maximize His son's impact on the earth. He will use a parental substitute to maximize your impact in the world as well. Substitute parental adoption doesn't heal you of prejection; instead it affords you a laboratory in which to work out and walk out the healing that has already taken place in you. But to accept a *SPA* and move to the next level of healing it offers, you must first recognize the previous SPA opportunities you rejected. **On the following page list the names of the people who sought to fill the void left by your rejecting parent. Next, write a short gratitude speech to be shared with each one. Beginning with the last first, call each one and express your gratitude for their effort to fill the parenting void in your life. Somewhere within the call articulate that you are ready to let them parent you.**

Chapter 20

Comfort

The first two G.R.A.C.E. steps are internally focused, but the last three are externally focused. Full healing is manifest when we are finally able to get our own pain, loss and anger off our minds and think about the welfare of someone else. Not because we've been forced or shamed into doing so, but because we're living out of the overflowing love of God in our own lives. When our souls get healed the love God sheds abroad in our hearts that used to seep out of our damaged souls will instead begin to fill our souls and spill over into others' lives. We will find *new desires and capacities* within for ministering to others.

Pain - can be a gift from Yahweh to help us bless the world. You'll be drawn to people in pain, with a new desire and capacity to help them.

Compassion - is about our ability to look past our own inconvenience in order to be moved with pity in our guts by and for someone else's pain. You'll have more compassion for prejects, and a greater capacity to be around them without wanting to run away.

True Comfort - is the presence of one called alongside to help who walks with us through our time and season of pain, reminding us that the pain will be productive, and helping us to endure it.

The following exercises will help you to focus your new desires and capacities to provide pain management, compassion, and true comfort.

- **Make a list of the people the Holy Spirit brings to your mind who are in pain, and also in your life's orbit.**
- **Next to each name describe the pain and its source.**
- **Ask the Holy Spirit to flash into your mind how you can help them get through the pain, and write what you see.**
- **Now follow through and do it.**

Comfort

Chapter 21

Establish

The Five Family Statements™

The final G.R.A.C.E. step is the *establishment* of one's own family, and here the distinction between establishing and making a family is monumental. *Making* a family is not enough because to make means to begin or start, and so a made family is still subject to failure or disintegration. For a family to endure, last forever, it must be *established* (to rise, stand erect). Only established families can make an impact for eternity, because they are dependable, standard.

It is really easy to make a family, but very difficult to establish one. Making a family only requires sperm and an egg. Establishing a family requires submission to a message and the living out of principles that are questioned and rejected because they are counter culture in a society that values family with lip service more than deed and truth. Establishing a loving, affirming, accepting family doesn't happen accidentally, nor overnight, but happens on purpose and requires time, intent, and a plan. Like the universe Yahweh versed, anything that is going to last forever must begin with a word, a statement. That is the purpose of the *Five Family Statements™*. Completing these exercises will help you to establish your family on words that will stand the test of time.

The following exercises and worksheets are provided to help you create your own *Five Family Statements™*. You may also visit *http://foodforfaith.org/5statements* for an online version of these worksheets that can be shared across the internet. This is especially useful for families with children away at college or busy, mobile teenagers at home.

Chapter 22

Establish

1. The Family Purpose Statement

Families are the ultimate *small group* and should be run like one, with the five *purposes* of the church, Yahweh's family, visible in the household. That means the family meets regularly (preferably daily around the breakfast and/or dinner table) and each purpose is *championed* by a different member of the family.

Families are organizations. The very first organization was a family (Adam & Eve, Cain & Abel). Organizational theory is birthed out of and defines family systems theory. Virtually every organization wants to be a *family*. *Food for Faith Publications* and *foodforfaith.org* helps organizations learn how to be family; functional family.

The five purposes of the church manifest in families are: (**s**ervice, **h**elps, **a**doration, **r**elationships, and **e**ducation). They should be visible in all the family statements, but especially in the *Family Purpose Statement*, because they are the DNA of the family Yahweh intended when He designed them.

- Purpose, vision, and mission are imparted, so these statements need to be created by the parents and shared with the children. Values and strategies are negotiated, so these statements need to be created collaboratively among parents and children.
- As families grow (numerically, developmentally, experientially, spiritually) values and strategies can and should change, but the family's purpose should always remain consistent.

The *Family Purpose Statement* should be no more than a paragraph long, and preferably a sentence long. The shorter the statement the easier to commit to memory and the more likely it is to be incorporated into the lifestyle of each family member.

The *Family Purpose Statement* should be a statement about why the family exists and/or what it exists to do. e.g.:

Family Purpose Statement - Sample
The Wrighter family exists to carry and demonstrate the grace of Yahweh, succeed at everything it attempts for Yahweh, and eloquently express the faith of Yahweh through word and deed.

Creating a Family Purpose Statement

1. What are the names of the people in your family?

_____
_____
_____
_____
_____

2. What do those names mean?

_____
_____
_____
_____
_____

3. Construct a sentence, utilizing the meanings of your family members' names, which expresses what you believe to be the reason why your family exists.

_____
_____
_____
_____
_____
_____

Chapter 23

Establish

2. The Family Vision Statement

Vision and sight are different. Vision is *imag-in-ation*; sight is *imag-out-ation*. The blind can have vision, while the seeing can lack imagination (*vision*). Vision is spiritual. Sight is physical. Adam and Eve had vision before they had or received sight. They were created visionaries who depended on vision to function and operate in the garden. The serpent got them to trade vision for sight, and humanity's been groping ever since, trying to feel our way through life with no vision. Feeling is what you do when you lack vision.

Yahweh intended Adam and Eve to live by faith (the ability to see inside what can't be seen. He wanted them to live by the pictures and sights He put *in* them, not around them. So, even though they could see what was around them, they saw it through the lens of what was *in* them.

A *Family Vision Statement* is a product of the family leaders' vision, not sight; thus it is spiritual, not physical. It requires leaders to pay attention to what they're seeing inside. It's harder to do in our visual culture because we are inundated by *serpents* hawking technological fruit, *carn*ival barkers calling attention to our carnal desires. Screens calling to our outer eyes are everywhere, disengaging our inner eye, overwhelming our inner vision. It's hard, but doable, and entirely necessary, even mandatory.

Without a *Family Vision Statement* all the children and parents will arrive at their own personal vision statements that will tear at the unifying fabric of the family and pull everyone in different directions with different agendas. Personally manufactured vision eventually leaves us unsatisfied and out of touch with Yahweh's will for our lives, but imparted vision leads us to wholeness.

The *Family Vision Statement* should be no more than a paragraph long, and preferably a sentence long. The shorter the statement the easier to commit to memory and the more likely it is to be incorporated into the lifestyle of each family member.

The *Family Vision Statement* should be a faith statement about the picture Yahweh has given the family to complete and/or maintain, and where the family will be existentially and functionally at a future point in time; i.e. where the family is headed. e.g.:

Family Vision Statement - Sample
The Wrighter family's vision is to build and operate a preject center in Los Angeles, by 2014, that will heal the damaged souls of people who have been rejected by their parents.

A full and complete vision statement will imply multiple phases of the vision so that even after the completion date there is still more left to do to fully satisfy the vision.

Creating a Family Vision Statement
1. What is the life vision given by Yahweh to the husband and father, the leader of the household?

_____
_____
_____

2. What is the life help vision given by Yahweh to the wife and mother, the co-leader of the household?

_____
_____
_____

3. Construct a sentence, utilizing the vision (the two visions must be one, or else the family will be divided by the experience of di-vision) of the parents, which expresses what you believe to be the current vision which was sent and assigned to your family.

_____
_____
_____

Chapter 24

Establish

3. The Family Mission Statement

Vision is for groups, mission is for individuals. A mission is an individual pursuit of a vision. A vision is sent by Yahweh to a group of people to get them from one place to another. It is meant for others to read and run with. The vision is the context for the mission. Yahweh gave Noah both a vision and a mission. His mission was to build an ark, but it was to serve the larger vision of establishing a new covenant with human life on the earth. I do my mission to fulfill my vision. Without a vision there is no course or destination for my mission. One must wait on Yahweh for the vision *and* the mission before one gets up to run and fulfill the vision by making up a mission of his own. If not, one will run blindly, without direction, wasting time and energy, and no doubt fail at the self-created mission and not fulfill the vision. The man and women must *wait* on their vision and their mission. The prophet Habakkuk went to his *watchtower* to look for and wait on a word from Yahweh before the word came. Adam was given both a vision and a mission when Yahweh placed him in the garden: keep the garden the way it is (vision) by tilling/cultivating/working the soil (mission).

The *Family Mission Statement* should be no more than a paragraph long, and preferably a sentence long. The shorter the statement the easier to commit to memory and the more likely it is to be incorporated into the lifestyle of each family member.

The Family Mission Statement should be a statement about what the family is assigned to do to fulfill its vision. e.g.:

Family Mission Statement - Sample
The Wrighter family's mission is to heal damaged souls by restoring people and families back to their originally intended design.

Creating a Family Mission Statement

1. What is the mission assigned by Yahweh to the husband and father, the leader of the household?

_____
_____
_____
_____
_____
_____
_____

2. What is the help mission assigned by Yahweh to the wife and mother, the co-leader of the household?

_____
_____
_____
_____
_____
_____
_____

3. Construct a sentence, utilizing the mission (the two missions must serve the same vision) of the parents, which expresses what you believe to be the mission for which your family was created (Yahweh creates families in the same way that He creates people—for a reason and with a plan in mind).

_____
_____
_____
_____
_____
_____

Chapter 25

Establish

4. The Family Values Statement

You want your *Family Values Statement* to be a useful tool, something that helps you to make decisions, and frees you up to say "no" to the things that aren't part of or consistent with it, even if it's a good thing — because for your family, it's just not the best thing, at least right at that moment.

Values are simply the concepts and ideals that hold the most valence, worth, or importance for a family. They are the tenets of belief and the shared perspectives that form the foundation for all our decisions, choices, and actions. Our core values list what experiences are most important to us.

The *Family Values Statement* should be no more than a page long, and preferably a bullet list of phrases no longer than a short sentence. The shorter the phrases the easier to commit to memory and the more likely they are to be incorporated into the lifestyle of each family member.

The *Family Values Statement* should be a listing of ideal behaviors and experiences that the family values, based on their understanding of their purpose and identity. e.g.:

> ***Family Values Statement - Sample***
> *The Wrighter family's core values are to:*
> - *Love Yahweh*
> - *Love Ourselves*
> - *Value Family Members*
> - *Nurture Deep Relationships*
> - *Love Our Neighbor*
> - *Live the Kingdom*

- *Manage Yahweh's Resources*
- *Learn Every Day*

Creating a Family Values Statement

1. Gather the family and ask each person (as much as they are able) to write down or share up to ten experiences that are most important to them; experiences they believe give their lives rich meaning and joy.

_____
_____
_____
_____
_____
_____
_____
_____
_____
_____

2. Compare and compile the lists, placing experiences matched by two or more at the top, and unmatched experiences at the bottom.

3. Compare the matched experiences to the family purpose statement, checking for consistency and agreement.

4. Eliminate all experiences that are inconsistent with the family purpose statement.

5. Reach consensus on unmatched experiences that are consistent with the family purpose statement.

6. Construct a list of no more than ten agreed upon ideal experiences that form the foundation of the family's decision-making and lifestyle.

_____
_____
_____
_____
_____
_____
_____
_____
_____
_____

Chapter 26

Establish

5. The Family Strategy Statement

A *Family Strategy Statement* maps out how a family plans to create and safeguard the experiences listed in its core values statement. It is helpful, even necessary, to depict the family's core values along with the family's strategy on the same document in order to visually remind everyone that the two are indivisibly linked. Values are just nice sentiments without a strategy to realize them; and strategies are just a list of activities without a set of values and goals to give them meaning and direction. In effect, a *Family Strategy Statement* is an amplification of the *Family Values Statement*. The value statement can be depicted by itself and still be useful, but the strategy statement can only be listed along with the value statement in order to have meaning.

The *Family Strategy Statement* should be no more than a page long, and preferably a bullet list of phrases no longer than a short sentence. The shorter the phrases the easier to commit to memory and the more likely they are to be incorporated into the lifestyle of each family member.

The *Family Strategy Statement* should be a listing of the actions and positions the family commits to in order to bring the ideal behaviors and experiences that the family values to pass consistently. e.g.:

Family Strategy Statement - Sample
The Wrighter family's strategy is to:
- *Love Yahweh*

- by regularly spending time with Him through His Word and in prayer
- by obeying His word despite the apparent cost
- by intentionally carrying His presence with us everywhere we go
- by telling others about Him when asked or given opportunity

- *Love Ourselves*
  - by eating foods our bodies were designed to eat
  - by avoiding toxic behaviors, products, and people
  - by doing regular cardio and resistance exercises
  - by taking time each day for an activity we enjoy
  - by taking care of ourselves before we take care of others
  - by regularly giving our bodies the rest and sleep they need

- *Value Family Members*
  - by excellently doing our chores without complaints
  - by helping each other when we see an opportunity
  - by feeling each other's emotions
  - by being quick to listen, slow to speak, and slow to get angry
  - by praying for each other publicly and privately

- *Nurture Deep Relationships*
  - by eating breakfast and dinner together
  - by honoring an at least weekly date time as a couple
  - by spending one-on-one time regularly, each parent with each kid, and each kid with each other
  - by honoring & guarding a weekly family game night
  - by regularly sharing our thoughts and feelings with each other on purpose
  - by communicating with each other daily either in person, by phone, by video chat, or by text

- *Love Our Neighbor*
  - by keeping our home tidy enough to welcome spontaneous guests
  - by helping strangers, even if it means welcoming them into our home

- *by hosting at least one family, couple, or individual for a meal per month who cannot return the gesture*
- *by regularly praying for our neighbors*
- *by looking for and seizing opportunities to help and bless others*

- **Live the Kingdom**
  - *by remaining completely debt-free at all times*
  - *by maintaining an emergency fund for our family*
  - *by sowing materially into each other's lives*
  - *by speaking only words of blessing over each other*
  - *by laying hands on each other to heal and bless*

- **Manage Yahweh's Resources**
  - *by returning 10% of all my income to Yahweh for His house and work*
  - *by respecting the living creation through using only what I need, recycling, replenishing, and helping to keep the planet clean*
  - *by partnering with animals when necessary to fulfill our vision*

- **Learn Every Day**
  - *by regularly reading quality books & articles*
  - *by regularly experiencing new things as a family*
  - *by exposing my eyes, ears, and heart only to edifying entertainment messages*
  - *by daily studying, honing and perfecting my craft*

Creating a Family Strategy Statement

1. Gather the family and ask each person (as much as they are able) to write down or share at least one *action* or *position* they are willing to commit to in order to bring about *each one* of the core values the family has agreed upon.

_____
_____
_____
_____
_____

2. Compare and compile the lists, placing actions and positions matched by two or more at the top, and unmatched actions and positions at the bottom.

3. Compare the matched actions and positions to the *Family Values Statement*, checking for consistency, agreement, and fulfillment potential.

4. Eliminate all experiences that are inconsistent with or will not fulfill the *Family Values Statement*.

5. Reach consensus on unmatched actions and positions that are consistent with and will fulfill the *Family Values Statement*.

6. Construct an outlined list of agreed upon actions and positions for each of the core family values, depicting them on one page.

Chapter 27

Establish

The Five Family Statements™

Application & Usage

- Create an 11x17 copy at your local print center (Kinko's, Office Depot, Staples, etc.) of the purpose, vision, and mission statements all on one page, in that order.
- Create an 11x17 copy at your local print center of the values and strategy statements all on one page.
- Post both documents in a visible location near the family breakfast and/or dinner table.
- Create an 8.5x11 copy of both documents for each family member and post them near each family member's bed.
- Create digital copies of both documents for each family member to use as wallpaper for computers, PDAs, and cell phones.
- Choose a consistent, monthly time to verbally review both documents with the entire family.
- Each New Year's Eve gather the family and consider revising the family statements, and each New Year's Day recommit as a family to honoring the five statements in your household.

Part 4

Signs

The Hallmarks of a PRO Life

- Orphaned Hearts & the Journey to Sonship
- Forty Parenting Skills for Prejects
- The Ten Commandments for Prejects

Chapter 28

Orphaned Hearts & the Journey to Sonship

Deconstructing Prejection

When a child is rejected by a parent (a prejecter), an orphan heart develops through that prejection and is visible anywhere the parent's love is absent or misunderstood. Here are some ways to tell if you are walking with an orphan heart, along with exercises to help you step into sonship:

1. *Performance over Presence* – Projects find it hard to be satisfied with Daddy Yahweh's presence because they had at least one parent who was never satisfied with their presence, so never taught them how to be satisfied with presence in a relationship. **Read the story of Mary & Martha in Luke 10:38-42 and list the contrasts between performance and presence.**

_____
_____
_____
_____
_____

2. *Trying* (it's up to me; my own efforts) – *Try* is the language and behavior of the fearful and unbelieving. It is what people do when they are afraid to make a commitment, or to put all their eggs in one basket and be disappointed. It is the hallmark of slavery and orphanhood. **Using**

a concordance, list all the instances of divine use of the word 'try' in scripture and their contextual definitions.

_____
_____
_____
_____
_____

3. *Striving* (at all costs to me and others) – Orphans have established residences on *Strivers Row* and believe they have to work for (or steal, which is itself a form of work) everything they get; that like the prodigal son, no one will give them anything good. **Using the four gospels, list all instances of Jesus depicted as working hard/overexerting himself to achieve results. Explain your findings.**

_____
_____
_____
_____
_____

4. *Fighting* (others; often over a legitimate wrong or slight) – Orphans are constantly fighting, and often over a legitimate wrong or slight. Orphans are super sensitive to injustice, even seeing it where it doesn't obviously exist. This is both a blessing and a curse. When an orphan's heart is healed s/he is able to *bless those who curse you* and stop fighting; but unhealed orphans fight. **Compare and contrast in detail your reaction to the last time you were wronged with Jesus' reaction to his trial and crucifixion.**

_____
_____
_____
_____
_____

5. *Territorial (competitive)* – The orphan heart is territorial because, being disconnected from Dad, it thinks it owns (or must work to own) everything. A connected son knows that everything belongs to Dad and, because he's an heir, he does not have to work for it to own it; it belongs to him, also. **Define Jesus' earthly goal. List his competitors. Did Jesus engage competition? Explain.**

Orphaned Hearts & the Journey to Sonship

_____
_____
_____
_____
_____

6. *Sealed Hearts* – We don't open up to people we don't trust. When an orphan seals his/her heart to keep it from further damage, like hardened PlayDoh®, it can no longer be molded to its original design or condition. Hearts were never meant to be hard, but pliable and resilient. **Detail the moment you decided to seal your orphaned heart against further damage. Now write a new decision to unseal it.**

_____
_____
_____
_____
_____

7. *Daddy Dependence* – There was a time in my past when I started a radio program, but couldn't build an audience. I believed I had no audience, in part, because I had no covering. I had no spiritual father authorizing my radio (or any other) ministry, and because I was so father hungry from daddy lack, I believed going into ministry with no father sending me out held me back from producing fruit. I had the mandate of the Father in heaven, but it wasn't enough. **List projects you gave up on because of failure you attributed to lack of a father's cover. Identify the first step needed to restart them. Restart them.**

_____
_____
_____
_____
_____

8. *Service Resentment* – Orphans hate to serve anyone but themselves, because they have all their lives equated service with bondage. Sonship doesn't obviate service, it contextualizes and redeems it; *real sons serve* alongside servants, the difference being that sons have an inheritance, and therefore, a different stake in the service. Servants serve *for* provision, while sons serve *from* it. **List any service opportunities you lost or abandoned because you equated them with bondage. Identify the first step necessary to reclaim them. Reclaim them.**

Chapter 29

40 Parenting Skills for Prejects

Parenting Prescriptions

Parental Reject Overcomer (PRO) parents are uniquely qualified to become the world's best parents because of the skills they acquire on the journey from healing to overcoming. Refer to the 40 PRO parenting skills in chapter 12 of *When My Mother & Father Forsake Me...*. Which of the 40 skills do you possess and function in proficiently? Which skills would be the most difficult for you to acquire on your own, and why? Conclude this section with a written prayer to Yahweh for help and direction in the acquisition of the skills you know are impossible for you to acquire on your own.

_____
_____
_____
_____
_____
_____
_____
_____
_____

Chapter 30

Ten Commandments for Prejects

Protecting Your Soul Health

One of the most destructive effects of prejection is its theft of parental honor from children, which makes life hard for prejects. Prejects who have completed their PRO journey have arrived at the place where they can deal with their parents from a spiritual place (absent feelings) rather than a sensitive one (where feelings and the senses rule – *Jude 19*). Prejects who have managed to recover parental honor are able to keep these *Ten Commandments for Prejects*, not as a matter of law and constraint, but from their heart:

1. *Get your soul healed and restored.* Healing happens instantaneously. Restoration takes a lifetime. The moment you release your parent, your soul gets healed. The moment you commit to living the five G.R.A.C.E. steps daily, restoration begins. **Record the date, time, and moment that both healing and restoration began for you.**

_____
_____
_____
_____
_____

2. *Protect your soul.* Because the soul is the container for the heart, it is vital to protect it so that it can do its job well: provide a safe environment for the heart. Soul protection requires soul maintenance. **List 7 protection verses of scripture and declare them over your soul daily.**

_____
_____
_____
_____
_____

3. *Build an overflow relationship with Yahweh.* The things that are impossible with men are possible with Yahweh *(Luke 18:27)*. It is impossible, in our flesh, to forget and overcome the rejection of a parent, which is the deepest betrayal imaginable. The only way to accomplish this is through a working, overflow relationship with Yahweh wherein His spirit powers us past our flesh to victory. **Using a concordance, find 7 bible verses that express God's promises to prejects. Transcribe them here, hide them in your heart, and confess them daily.**

_____
_____
_____
_____
_____
_____
_____
_____
_____

4. *Pray for your parents daily.* Many prejects are trying to erase their parents *out* of their minds. The way to healing requires we put them *in* our minds by praying *for* them! When you pray *for* your parents, blessing them that curse (limit or hinder) you, and doing good to them that hate you, you behave like a child of Yahweh (and begin to prosper). **Using the specific circumstances of your prejection, write a prayer of blessing for your rejecting parent(s), then begin to offer it daily.**

5. *Look for and take a faith risk daily.* One sign of preject healing and health is the ability to take faith risks. Prejects are too consumptive to step out of (extend) themselves to take a faith risk (which is different than a *faith* gamble: we risk from fullness, but we gamble from emptiness). **Record in detail a faith risk you will take every day, then, like Peter, step out of your boat!**

6. *Sow a seed daily.* We sow seeds to reap harvests. The process is an intentional investment in our future. It takes a sense of optimism about the future to be bearish and invest in it. When we have a sense of foundation in the present, which is what parental honor brings us, we are able to look at the future with hope and optimism. Honoring parents leads to sowing from the heart. **Identify and record in detail what kind of daily harvest you want in your life, then write a prayer asking God for good ground and daily seed to sow for that daily harvest.**

7. *Help another preject daily.* Recognizing our own pain in someone else requires some distance from our own experience, and then assisting that person through their pain requires some personal knowledge or the roadmap through it. None of this is possible if we are still overcome and overwhelmed by our own pain. Once we've been liberated, it will be and

feel natural for us to reach to and help liberate others enduring the same pain. **Make a list of all the prejects you know of in your life, and next to each name write at least one way you will help them.**

___

8. *Accept and nurture a child daily.* When we've been damaged by rejection and a lack of nurture, we develop a heightened awareness of what real acceptance and nurture look like, and so are best able to picture it, project it, and impart it to others once we've been healed ourselves. Offering others what we've never received is one way to connect with it. **Make a list of all the children in your life. Next to each name describe an act of acceptance and nurture you will demonstrate to that child.**

___

9. *View or hear a preject prescription daily.* Healing is only one (and the first) stage of the overcoming process. The final and longest stage is maintenance, and it requires filling our ears and hearts with the message that liberates us. Preject prescriptions are available daily via our online *G.R.A.C.E. Steps* videos, and are the best way to maintain a PRO attitude. **Create a daily schedule that you can stick to for viewing preject prescriptions.**

10. *Thank Yahweh for your life daily.* Gratitude is only possible when we realize how much worse things could be for us, and how much better things are right now than they used to be at one point in our lives. A person who has overcome parental rejection will be grateful from their hearts for what Yahweh has done, and practice articulating that gratitude daily. **Write a gratitude speech to Yahweh, thanking Him for all the good things and benefits in your life that you can think of.**

Appendix

Audio/Video Resources for Healing Parental Rejection & Hurts

Available at *www.foodforfaith.org*:

1. *The Healing Parental Rejection & Hurts CD Audio Series.* Ten sessions taught by A. Jesus Wrighter, focusing on the Five G.R.A.C.E. Steps™. Study guides available. (*Food for Faith Publications*)

2. *The Healing Parental Rejection & Hurts DVD Series.* Ten sessions taught by A. Jesus Wrighter, focusing on the Five G.R.A.C.E. Steps™. Study guides available. (*Food for Faith Publications*)

3. *Heal Your Cistern CD.* How to heal your cistern-soul and enjoy the full life you were designed to live. (*Food for Faith Publications*)

4. *Cracking the Code of Silence.* Six-CD audio program on breaking the silence that prevents real intimacy in households and relationships. (*Food for Faith Publications*)

5. *Fine Church Girls: Season 1.* The internet's first Christian dramedy series featuring four preject women in a small group. (*Food for Faith Productions*)

Free Resources

E-mail *prejectnews@foodforfaith.org* for a free subscription to the monthly online *Healing Parental Rejection & Hurts* newsletter.

E-mail *gracesteps@foodforfaith.org* for a free subscription to *G.R.A.C.E. Steps*, the daily online devotional for people healing from parental rejection and hurts.

Visit *www.ThePrejectTest.com* for a free self-assessment to determine the condition of your soul as a result of the impact of your parental relationships.

About the Author

A. Jesus Wrighter is a former pastor who has been estranged from his parents for many years. After graduating from Princeton Theological Seminary he was promptly voted out of two pastorates. However, in January of 1996 he heard the audible voice of God while driving home in the family minivan after dropping his daughter off at school. It was only one word, but it was clear: WRITE! It took him several years to finally obey that word, but today he is the author of a growing catalog of fiction and non-fiction titles, most of them dealing with the power of God's G.R.A.C.E. to heal and restore souls damaged by any form of parental rejection. Most important of all, he has found healing, wholeness, full acceptance, and unconditional love in his relationship with his Heavenly Father through Jesus Christ.

Send Us Your Story!

Stories change lives. Those of the hearers and the tellers. Our story is our *testimony* of what we've personally experienced, or seen and heard in someone else's life. One of the ways the people of Yahweh overcome adversity is through the word of their *testimony*.[1] Perhaps you have a story about how you, or someone you know or have heard of, overcame an aspect of parental rejection by applying one or more of the Five G.R.A.C.E. Steps™. If you'd like to share your story with us, and have it considered for possible inclusion in a future book, please send it to:

Food for Faith Publications
G.R.A.C.E. Stories
P.O. Box 88445
Los Angeles, CA 90009
E-mail: *gracestories@foodforfaith.org*

About Food for Faith Publications™

Food for Faith Publications™ is a Christian teaching and publishing ministry. The buzzword in the media world is 'content,' and its new frontier is the internet. We believe Yahweh has given us a mandate to publish the gospel in every arena using all available means. We are doing our part to get God's content into the new frontier in a techno-friendly format.

Food for Faith Publications™ mission is to reconnect people to God through His word.

Food for Faith Publications™ publishes content that helps people build an intelligent relationship with God.

If you're interested in ordering additional copies of this workbook for your school, send an e-mail to *schools@foodforfaith.org*.

If you're interested in ordering additional copies of this workbook for your church, send an e-mail to *churches@foodforfaith.org*.

You can also access *Food for Faith Publications*™ other products and services online at *www.foodforfaith.org*.

---

[1] *Revelation 12:11* (KJV) And they overcame him by the blood of the Lamb, and by the word of their testimony; and they loved not their lives unto the death.

> If this book ministered to you, recommend *The AntiChrist Was Conceived in Queens* to your child or youth group!

The AntiChrist Was Conceived in Queens

What happens when a son kills his father...
and then tries to raise him from the dead?

 A. Jesus Wrighter

He's the product of an ancient, unholy union. She's a pawn in a high stakes, prophetic game of deception. When he accidentally kills his father an avalanche of unforeseen circumstances turns their worlds upside down and threatens the ultimate salvation of an entire species. Will a miracle resurrection be enough to restore order to his universe now spun out of control? And will *their* baby turn out to be the AntiChrist?

In a heart stopping romp through the streets of New York City, *The AntiChrist Was Conceived in Queens* manages to carve out a new genre, the BUFF novel (biblical urban faith fantasy), while following the transformation of Rain Reynolds, a New York City public school legend with real angel's blood in his veins, and Lisa Vickers, a former D.C. anchorwoman turned pastor with a secret, from immortal basketball icon and crack investigator to enlightened spiritual emissaries and perhaps their kind's last real hope to find a place in heaven. And as usual the way to enlightenment goes straight through the dark.

"The writing sings!"

"Finally a biblical faith novel your sons & husbands will read, too."

"An unforgettable story of one teen's struggle with parental rejection, on earth and in heaven, that will make you want to be the best parent, and best child, possible."

"A classic story of loss and redemption painted with masterful prose against a hardscrabble canvas."

> **Available Now!**
> at
> *www.foodforfaith.org*

Made in United States
North Haven, CT
12 July 2022